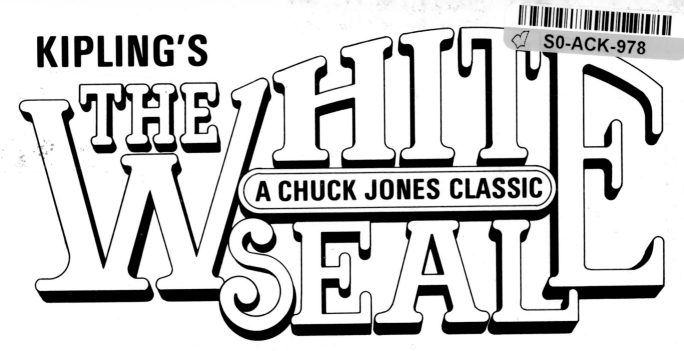

KIPLING'S THE WHITE SEAL

A CHUCK JONES CLASSIC

Ideals Publishing Corp.
Milwaukee, Wisconsin

Copyright © MCMLXXXII Chuck Jones Enterprises
Based upon a Motion Picture Film
© MCMLXXV Chuck Jones Enterprises.
All rights reserved. Printed and bound in U.S.A.

ISBN 0-8249-8042-5

All these things happened years ago at a place called Novastoshnah on the Island of Saint Paul, away and away in the Bering Sea.

Nobody comes to Novastoshnah except on business, and the only people who have regular business there are the seals—and those who hunt the seals.

The seals come in the summer months by hundreds of thousands out of the cold gray sea. Novastoshnah has the finest beaches for seals of any place in all the world.

Sea Catch knew that and every spring would swim from whatever place he happened to be straight for Novastoshnah and would spend a month fighting with his companions for a good place on the rocks as close to the sea as possible.

Sea Catch was fifteen years old, a huge gray fur-seal. He stood more than four feet clear of the ground, and his weight, if anyone had been bold enough to weigh him, was nearly seven hundred pounds.

Sea Catch only wanted room by the sea for his nursery. Unfortunately there were forty or fifty thousand other seals hunting for the same thing each spring. The whistling, bellowing, roaring, and blowing on the beach were something frightful.

The wives never came to the island until late in May or early in June.

Sea Catch had just finished his forty-fifth fight one spring when Matkah, his soft, sleek, gentle-eyed wife, came up out of the sea.

"Late, as usual," Sea Catch gruffed. "Where have you been?"

Matkah paid no attention to his temper, looked around and cooed, "How thoughtful of you! You've taken the old place again."

"I haven't been doing anything but fight for it since the middle of May," Sea Catch grumbled. "The beach is disgracefully crowded this season. I've met at least a hundred seals from Lukannon Beach."

"You do provide such a beautiful nursery for our babies every year," said Matkah. "You are a wonderful husband, and father, too."

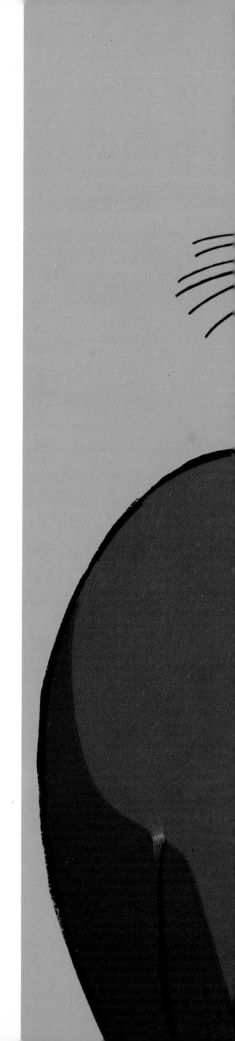

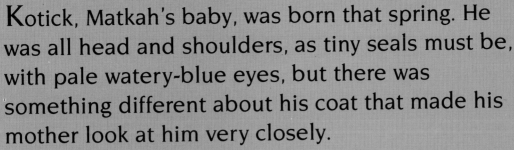

Kotick, Matkah's baby, was born that spring. He was all head and shoulders, as tiny seals must be, with pale watery-blue eyes, but there was something different about his coat that made his mother look at him very closely.

"Sea Catch," she said at last, "I do believe our baby is going to remain white!"

"Empty clamshells and dry seaweed!" snorted Sea Catch. "There never has been such a thing as a white seal."

"I can't help that," said
Matkah. "There is going to be
one now." She sang the low,
crooning seal-song all mother
seals sing to their babies:

You must not swim till you're six weeks old,
  Or your head will be sunk by your heels;
And summer gales and killer whales
  Are bad for baby seals,

Are bad for baby seals, my dear,
  As bad as bad can be;
But splash and grow strong,
  And you can't be wrong,
Child of the open sea!

Of course, the little fellow did
not understand the words at first.

Little seals can no more swim than little children, but they are unhappy till they learn. The first time that Kotick went down to the sea a wave carried him out beyond his depth, and his big head sank and his little hind flippers flew up exactly as his mother had told him in the song. If Matkah had not buoyed him up, he would have drowned.

After that he learned to lie in a beach-pool and let the wash of the waves just cover him and lift him up while he paddled, but he always kept his eye open for big waves that might hurt.

It took Kotick weeks to learn how to use his flippers. All that while he floundered in and out of the water and coughed and grunted and crawled up on the beach and took naps on the sand, and went back again until ...

… at last, he found that he truly belonged to the water—that he belonged to the sea not the land.

From that moment on, he lived in the water, ducking under the rollers or coming in on top of a comber and landing with a swash and a splutter as the big wave went whirling far up the beach.

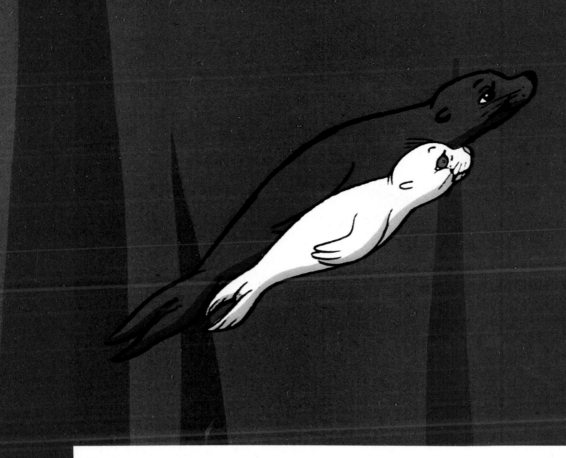

Late in October the seals leave Saint Paul for the deep sea. The powerful bulls, quite warm in their layers of skin, spend the winter in the icy Alaskan waters while the mothers and their young swim thousands of miles south, past San Francisco, as far south as San Diego and Mexico.

Matkah and Kotick bid Sea Catch good-bye and set out together across the Pacific. There Matkah showed Kotick how to sleep on his back; for no cradle is as comfortable as the long, rocking swell of the Pacific.

This was one of the very many things Kotick learned, and he was always learning. Matkah taught him to follow the cod and the halibut along the undersea banks. She showed him how to wrench the rockling out of his hole among the reeds.

And before leaving him to learn to survive alone, she taught him how to skirt the shipwrecks lying a hundred fathoms below water and dart like a rifle-bullet in at one porthole and out at another to escape from the seal's terrifying enemy—the shark!

The shark, however, was not the seal's *most* terrifying enemy!

One day Kotick saw a strange but harmless-looking sea-creature. As he swam out to greet it, he noticed he was not moving forward—his mother had taken hold of his back flippers.

"Kotick!" scolded Matkah. "I leave you alone for a few weeks, and you almost lose your life. Never! Never ever stop to look at a boat!"

"A boat?" asked Kotick, amazed. "Are boats bad—like sharks?"

"Boats carry men," said Matkah, "and men are the most terrible, the most pitiless enemies seals will ever know."

"How can I keep away from them?" asked Kotick. "How will I know them when I see them?"

"You will know them, my darling," his mother answered sadly, "because they will be dressed in the skins of dead seals," and she gathered him tightly to her breast.

By the end of six months on his own, without setting a flipper on dry land and seeing boats only at great distances, Kotick had lost all fear of that mysterious thing called man. He had grown enormously and was absolutely certain that what he did not know about the sea was not worth knowing.

As he headed the seven thousand miles north to Novastoshnah, Kotick met many other young bachelors—or holluschickie as they are called— all bound for the same place.

Hutchinson's Hill was the playground of the holluschickie. It was located well away from the beach of the fighting bulls. There the holluschickie practiced the games that would make them strong enough to fight some day.

"What a wonderful life!" thought Kotick as he bounded up the hill. "The happiest thing in the world is to be a holluschickie;" and he dove right into a snowbank.

Just then the holluschickie became aware of a noise which grew louder and louder until its source came into view. Men wearing fur coats and rattling kerosene tins stomped toward the holluschickie.

The seals, at first surprised and then frightened, backed away in front of them, and were gradually driven farther inland.

Blending into the snow with his white fur, Kotick was able to escape the men whom he now knew to be seal hunters. His mother's words echoed in his ears: "They will be dressed in the skins of dead seals."

Kotick dashed as fast as he could back to the main herd, calling, "Quickly! Come quickly! The men are driving all the holluschickie away!" Catching his breath, he cried, "I think they're going to skin them! You can't *live* without skin!"

The fighting bulls barely roused themselves from slumber to say, "Oh, the men do that to a few every year. What's a few young bulls more or less?"

Kotick was speechless! Everyone was ignoring the holluschickie's plight. "What's a few young bulls?" he said. "They are my friends!"

Alone, Kotick galloped back to the playground and beyond, hoping there was some way he could save his friends. As he approached a cliff overlooking a pit aglow with firelight, his heart stood still. Below him, the holluschickie were backed against the cliff wall and were surrounded by men holding clubs.

As the men raised their clubs, Kotick's fear turned to anger, and he barked, "STOP IT! STOP IT! STOP IT! STOP IT!"

His voice echoed off the cliffs and startled the hunters who looked away from the helpless holluschickie and up at Kotick, the white seal. An enormous black shadow created by the fire's glow set off Kotick's gleaming white coat.

"It can't be!" said one hunter. "It's a white seal!"

"No! There is no such thing!" said another.

"Then it must be a ghost!" said a third. "It's the ghost of all the seals we've ever killed come to haunt us! Run!"

"Run! Run!" the hunters all cried fearfully. Kotick bellowed and barked angrily after them as they fled the island to their ship.

"I suppose it is rather awful from your way of looking at it," said Sea Vitch, the long-tusked walrus of the North Pacific, next morning. "But if you seals come here year after year, of course the men get to know of it. Unless you can find an island where no men ever come, you will always be driven."

"Isn't there any island — any place we can go and be safe?" asked Kotick.

"Go and ask the sea cow," Sea Vitch replied. "He would have been killed long ago if he had no safe place to go during the hunting season. If he's alive, he'll know where such an island is."

"But how shall I recognize the sea cow?" asked Kotick.

"I'm forced to admit," replied Sea Vitch, "he is the only one in the sea uglier than I am."

That very day Kotick left the beaches of
Novastoshnah in search of the sea cow and, of
course, the perfect island—with good firm
beaches on which seals could live and where men
could not come with clubs.

Kotick searched for five long years, questioning
friendly animals of the sea wherever he traveled.
He went to the great, barren Galapagos Islands ...

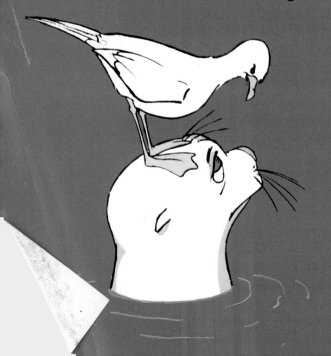

... to the Georgia Islands
and the South Orkneys ...

… Emerald Island, Little Nightingale Island, and McMurdo Sound …

… and even the dry Tortugas. But everywhere the story was the same—seals had come to those islands at one time, and men had killed them off.

Kotick had all but given up hope when one day
he came up for a breath of air after a long dive
and nearly bumped into a creature of the sea
which *was* uglier than the walrus.

"By the great combers of Magellan!" said
Kotick, "Sea Vitch was right!"

At last he had found the sea cow! But when
Kotick tried to question him about his secret
island, he discovered the sea cow could not
speak. It seemed all this creature could do all day
was float and munch and slurp away on seaweed.

Kotick settled down to wait for the time when the sea cow would leave for his special island, if there was one.

Sitting and watching the sea cow slowly munch and chump his way through the seaweed was almost enough to make Kotick's temper go where the dead crabs go.

Then one night, weeks later, the sea cow suddenly sank down into the water and, to Kotick's surprise, swam quickly—so quickly that it was all Kotick could do to keep up with him.

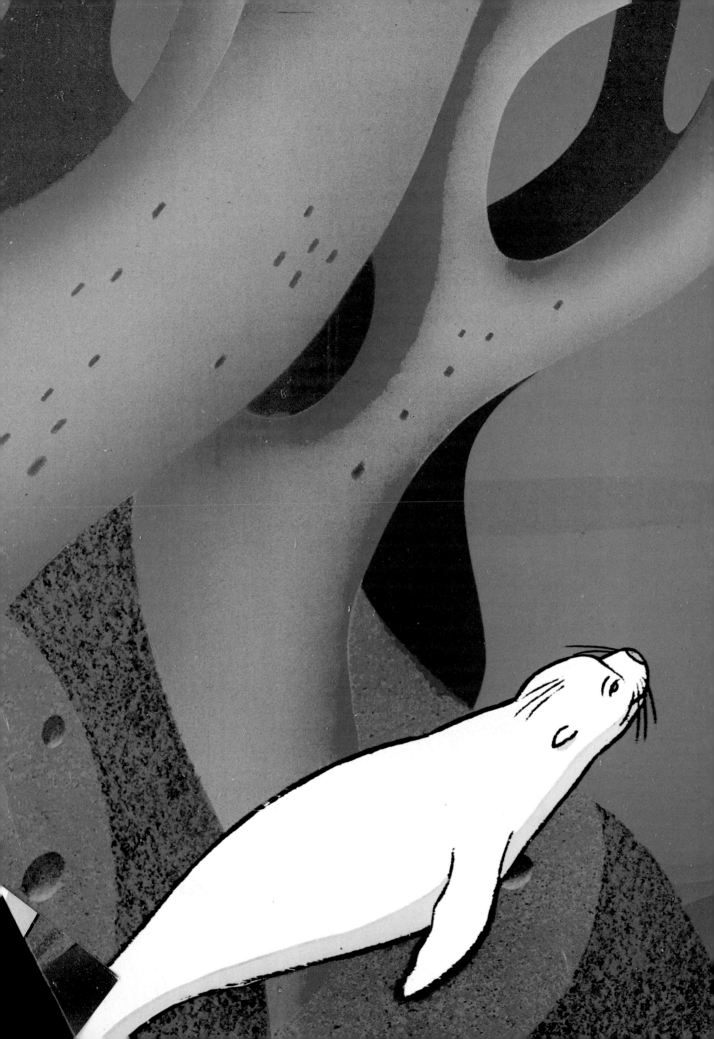

Every year, year after year, more and more seals came to these quiet, sheltered coves, these sun-struck beaches where Kotick sits all summer getting bigger and stronger and fatter each year, and where happy children play all around him in the golden sea—where no man comes.